MISSION
CATASTROPHE

Gloucestershire

Edited By Jenni Harrison

First published in Great Britain in 2019 by:

Young Writers
Remus House
Coltsfoot Drive
Peterborough
PE2 9BF
Telephone: 01733 890066
Website: www.youngwriters.co.uk

FOREWORD

Young Writers was created in 1991 with the express purpose of promoting and encouraging creative writing. Each competition we create is tailored to the relevant age group, hopefully giving each student the inspiration and incentive to create their own piece of work, whether it's a poem or a short story. We truly believe that seeing their work in print gives students a sense of achievement and pride in their work and themselves.

Our Survival Sagas series, starting with Mission Catastrophe and followed by Mission Contamination and Mission Chaos, aimed to challenge both the young writers' creativity and their survival skills! One of the biggest challenges, aside from facing floods, avoiding avalanches and enduring epic earthquakes, was to create a story with a beginning, middle and end in just 100 words!

Inspired by the theme of catastrophe, their mission was to craft tales of destruction and redemption, new beginnings and struggles of survival against the odds. As you will discover, these students rose to the challenge magnificently and we can declare *Mission Catastrophe* a success.

The mini sagas in this collection are sure to set your pulses racing and leave you wondering with each turn of the page: are these writers born survivors?

CONTENTS

Meerab Tahir (12)	66
Malindi Maughan (11)	67
Olivia Hopwood (13)	68
Diana Philip (11)	69
Ana Navarro-Garcia (11)	70

Rendcomb College School, Rendcomb

Bertie Parkes (12)	71
Henry Carr (12)	72
Thomas Henry George (13)	73
Edward Sweeney (13)	74
Chloe Witt (13)	75

Wyedean School, Sedbury

Lara Mueller (15)	76
Seán Hart (15)	77
Shannyn Hoare (12)	78
Lourdes Mann (12)	79
Gabriella Watkins (11)	80
Faye Martin (11)	81
Megan Lilly Sweet (12)	82
Idris McKie (12)	83
Emily Grace Burke (13)	84
Alice Morgan (12)	85
Georgia Watkin-Jones (12)	86
Samantha Grace Williamson (11)	87
Carys Martin (12)	88
Isabelle Walker (11)	89
Archie Underwood (11)	90
James Hardinge (11)	91
Harry Graham (11)	92
Chloe Susan Dolan (12)	93
Ethan Joseph Wood (12)	94
Jack Newman (11)	95
Charlie Howells (12)	96
Sam Cantle (11)	97
Caitlin Paige Firmin (11)	98
Lucas Bowen (12)	99
Georgia Huson (12)	100
Devon Powell (12)	101

Ioan Day (11)	102
Charlie Peter Steven Bethell (11)	103
Caitlin Jennings (13)	104
Jasmine Fellows (11)	105
Amber Morgan (11)	106
Alex Bint (15)	107
Hannah Gibson (12)	108
Florence Lily Hills (11)	109
Lacy-Mai Bollen (11)	110
Matthew Whitcombe (11)	111
Ethan Dash (12)	112
Todd Michael Thomas (11)	113
Liam Morgan (12)	114
Evie Rose Hunter (12)	115
Olivia Abigail Legg (11)	116
Jonah Ford (13)	117
Murray King (11)	118
Harriet Tyldesley (11)	119
Alexander Catlin (12)	120
Jack Qualter Buncall (12)	121
Abi Giles (11)	122
Izzy Robb (11)	123
Rhia Admans (12)	124
William Tett (12)	125
Phoebe Jones (12)	126
Fraser Rickards (11)	127
Will Haywood (11)	128

THE MINI SAGAS

Beautifully Broken World

"Get her!" snarled the man.

He died quickly. I was surprisingly merciful today.

"Help!"

My head turned towards the sound... My mind raced...

"Elizabeth!" I screamed.

I ran faster than the wind as I sprinted towards the office. Blood covered my dagger as I killed my way to her. Hundreds of officers crowded around me. Many died instantly but the ones I recognised... well, I lingered on them. I reached the door and flung it open. I was forced to watch as a machine gun shattered her, catching me in the line of fire. My vision went red.

"Avenge me."

Rudi Harward (12)
Archway School, Paganhill

One Day

I was walking. Little did I know that my life would change forever. Alarms were ringing.

"Get down!"

They were here, the terrorists. The warning level had been at high risk for ages now. I just thought it would never happen to me.

Bang! The gunshots were getting louder. I was hiding in the toilets. Why here? This was the worst place to be. The gunshots were practically right next to me.

"I know you're in here..." the stranger's voice echoed.

This was it, I was dead.

"I won't hurt or harm you, but only if you come out..."

Lara McEvoy (13)
Archway School, Paganhill

Missing

It has been two months since the 'occurrences'. People started going missing. They went missing in tens, hundreds, then thousands and billions. I'm living in this empty adoption home with ten other kids and one adult. We don't go outside, we all live in fear that we will go missing if we go outside. Our skin is pale and our clothes are dirty and grey. All emotions have been submerged to nothing, nobody speaks and our bedrooms are like cells. I've forgotten everything, our names, who we are and even what happened. I don't know what to do, I forgot.

Vivienne Green (12)
Archway School, Paganhill

Lifeless

There was no life left on Earth. Slowly, everyone would die. To try and make matters easier, the heavens above opened and started raining. Everyone gathered the water to try and live for a bit longer.

The attack from outer space was successful, the bombs destroyed everything. Everything was grey and dull. Everyone was miserable. There was no hope... I sipped the last drop of water from my cup. My eyes were about to close, they wouldn't hold much longer.

Before I went, I muttered to myself, "Why did they have to do this?"

My eyes gave way. I died.

Harry Peter Adey Weaver (13)
Archway School, Paganhill

Set Free

I squint my eyes, trying to see through the mist. I hear chainsaws and guns in the distance. I can see him, crooked-neck man. I don't know who he is, but he has a crooked neck and carries an axe.
The government set all prisoners free, saying that in the bible it says to give everyone a second chance.
He's there. I start running, I don't know where to, but I just run. Around every corner, there's a killer. I trip, there's no time for me to get up, there's no escape... An axe hovers over my head, death.

Amelia Andrews (13)
Archway School, Paganhill

The Final Klaxon

The burning scream of the final klaxon washed over the campsite. They were here and there was no escape. They heard the metal screws march, like toy soldiers. It went quiet, dead quiet. All they could hear was their own breathing. Vert's eyes poised at a hanging branch in the forest ahead. She blinked and the branch fell. The rows of moving machinery charged towards their tents. Their shine and rust cracked as they pierced the thumping flesh of the human's chest. Vert ran, but nowhere was safe... She met the end of a shotgun.

Annise Pomeroy (13)
Archway School, Paganhill

The Day After War

It all started after the war, food ran out. Towns were drowning from floods, some of us survived and built a sanctuary on water. Acid from all the unfortunate people who died from the floods made the water poisonous and fatal to drink. The only way to eat or drink was to drink our urine. We have been living like this for six years, but I got used to it about three years ago, after people realised the flood would stay. Countries and cities began fighting for boats and floating land. London was the leader and killed many other cities.

Tom Beauchamp (13)
Archway School, Paganhill

Burnt From The Ground

I put the lid on the spray can and sighed. Who else was still alive? Many more thoughts swam the lonely depths of my mind, questions mostly. I hoped it was the last of the infection. The realisation of what had just happened sank in and my knees buckled. I was alone now... I had no one. Tears glazed my eyes, blurring my vision. I let a few slip before completely breaking down. The acid virus completely swallowed my land, burning anything it touched. I rubbed the ash around me, letting it slip through my fingers gently. What now?

Alex Ansell (13)
Archway School, Paganhill

The Other Side

The little men were here. Everyone thought it was a meteor but I knew what it really was.

However, I'm the freak that everyone fears, yet I am safe. The world is under threat and I'm the only one who can save us. Suddenly, I hear a crash from above my underground bunker. Screams and shouts from armless people. The sound of flames and houses collapsing. I have the book that my parents gave to me the day that they died. Everyone is against me apart from the people that have recently arrived, who I believe are my own.

Felicity McColl (12)
Archway School, Paganhill

World War Three

I was walking home, as I normally do from school, past Blackberry power station. I heard a crash so, me being me, I had to walk into what I later found out was massive danger.
I stepped into the power plant, which was abandoned from what I could see. I reached for my penknife. Everything had gone silent. I was scared for the first time in my life; I didn't get a thrill of excitement. Then from behind a tree stepped a man. He stared at me with a strong gaze.
I stared back and said, "I will hurt you!"

Sarah March (12)
Archway School, Paganhill

Zombies!

It was a cold, frosty morning in Sweden. I was strolling down the street whilst walking my German shepherd called Lily. I was doing my usual dog route, past the graveyard and up the big hill. As I walked past the old creepy graveyard, I saw that all the graves had been dug up. I suddenly saw a strange man approaching me and my dog. I could hear him muttering something under his breath. As he got closer, my dog started ferociously barking at him. All of a sudden, twenty other people came near us. They were zombies!

Bethany Brennan Hulme (12)
Archway School, Paganhill

Survivor

I'm the only one left. All of my friends were taken. This is all my fault. They died, and... and there's nothing I can do about it. Oh no! They've found me, I still don't know what they are. I've been studying them for years now. I mean, since my dad got murdered. What I *do* know is they can only be killed by a silver bullet. What was that? I think it was a scream. There it is again. Maybe my friends are still alive...

Rosie Fuller (12)
Archway School, Paganhill

Humans Are The Real Monsters

It's been three days since I saw my parents get shot and I moved to the camp. I still can't believe all of the events that have happened in the past month. From the tsunami, to the earthquake, multiple buildings collapsed and my parents were shot. It's been awful but I have to find my brother. We've been trapped in this camp for a while and every day we are made to train to fight. It's like it was all planned...

Coco Mobley (12)
Archway School, Paganhill

The Inevitable

War was here. Everywhere. I couldn't stop it. I couldn't focus, and it was his fault... It bubbled up inside me, taking control. The magic fueled by anger and defeat. *She's okay, she's okay.* But he was still out there, his army too, hunting, searching for me.

The beauty of it. War. One country surrendering to another. His to mine.

"Sir! Your majesty! Sir!"

"Yes, general, what is it? This'd better not be a waste of my time."

"Our spies have been successful, we have found his location, and..."

"What?"

"We believe he has magic."

"No. No, no!"

Daisy Cameron (12)
High School For Girls, Gloucester

Saviour

"You, you knew them."

The words accusatory, barely audible.

"You didn't stop them."

The distant screams faded, a dull ringing was throbbing through my skull like air-raid sirens. I stumbled, legs shaking, lacerated with tendrils of red. Blood trickled off my fingertips. I stared past the broken figures ahead; they merged into the heat and the red sky. My eyes burning with tears that wouldn't come. My head pounded. The splintered remnants of my sanity waved just out of reach.

"But they..." my voice cracked, a fractured smile crossed my lips, "they were going to save the world."

Leah Mulligan (14)

High School For Girls, Gloucester

The Darkened Wilderness

"No!" screamed someone in agony.

The lunar eclipse had taken over every inch of daylight in the city. Transforming vivid streets into a darkened wilderness. Unbeknown to the inhabitants, this was not just any lunar eclipse, it transformed residents into frenzied, mouth-foaming lunatics. Microscopic rays of light enranged their senses and played tricks with their minds. Nothing could stop them, well almost nothing... Scarlett Stimpton, from the fifth precinct, began to stride down Hansdown Avenue, her red hair flowing in the gentle breeze. The glint in her eye presented a sense of confidence, as she met the marching lunatics.

Lilia Grace Morley (11)
High School For Girls, Gloucester

Sinister Creatures

An intoxicating aroma surrounded me. I was in detention. Just me. It was so addicting. Just then, my head started swinging and I woke up. There wasn't a soul around. Suddenly, a sensation penetrated through me, as if someone was breathing. Terror, horror and fear strangled me. Without looking back, I ran and discovered the darkest secret. They were watching the whole time. The earthquake, it was them!
Now is their chance to destroy humanity. Now they're after me. Oh god! The footsteps, they're coming closer. What do I do?
Wait, this isn't right. Something's wrong, something is *very* wrong...

Khadija Dilnawaz (13)
High School For Girls, Gloucester

Alien Invasion

Bang! The sound echoed across the mansion, entering rapidly, creating an ear-piercing sound in the mini arcade. Andrew and Zara looked around as they got up. Small debris from the ceiling floated around them, ruining their youthful lungs. They breathed in oxygen that was once fresh. Andrew saw blood everywhere, it destroyed him so much that he wanted to hurt himself. Everyone but them was gone.

"What do we do now?" he asked, grabbing any resources he could find around him.

"Andrew... Look behind you," whispered Zara.

He turned around to see millions of creatures coming towards him.

Cinta May Vincent (13)
High School For Girls, Gloucester

The End Of The World

As I opened my eyes, I could see my mum staring at me.

"Quick! Get up and pack your clothes!" exclaimed Mum eagerly.

Bewildered, I asked, "Why?"

Without a reply, I started to stuff my clothes into my bag.

Rushing down the stairs, my mum was waiting by the door for me with her suitcase.

"What took you so long, Polly? Hurry up!"

Rushing, Mum opened the door. People were sprinting in every direction. Everyone was heading to the nearest bunker.

"The meteor is heading to Earth in five minutes."

Not knowing what to do, my eyes began to close.

Ayesha Salehbhai (11)
High School For Girls, Gloucester

Zero Gravity

Her name was Nova Parrage. With a name like that, how could she be ordinary? She stared at the barren wasteland that was once called home. Nothing was ordinary anymore.

Nova was fifteen when the news arrived through subtle rumours, but gradually it spread until news reports thickly smothered the TV. *Gravity to be inexistent, none to survive.* Ancient trees and buildings ripped from the frosty ground, empowered by a ghostly grasp. Nora clung on to her father's trembling hand, desperate to tow him down. The air grew thinner, the atmosphere vanishing. She watched her life soar out of reach...

Dulcie Davidson (12)
High School For Girls, Gloucester

Seconds Too Late

"Government calls for immediate backup in the USA. Meanwhile, all citizens are advised to take shelter in homes, stores or other local buildings." Alan stared out of the window, his lips slightly parted in a subconscious effort to seize his surprise.

"Dad!" his daughter called, her eight-year-old body slumped on the plush sofa.

He wanted to protect his daughter, but right now all he saw, all he was fixated on, were the perilous screams outside. His lip slightly brushed against the curtain. Debris shot through the sky. He ran to his daughter but he was seconds too late.

Rio Lucy Snow (12)
High School For Girls, Gloucester

Technology Catastrophe!

Bill Watkinson was the one and only brain whizz of Oxford University. He held awards for practically anything imaginable. Until now. He created a robot that cleans, or so he thought...

Just yesterday, the world met its doom with only a few lucky survivors. The robot was thought to have escaped the warehouse and come out in the night, vandalising everything in sight, leaving nothing. At the speed of light, the robot used its artificial intelligence, copied its own programming and sent it to all computers around the world. Slowly and mercilessly, the evil robots consumed everything in sight...

Raneem Umar (11)

High School For Girls, Gloucester

The Switch

She was waiting, always waiting. Never knowing, always guessing, nonchalant of the dangers that awaited her. Glancing up, she did a retake as the building quivered. *This isn't supposed to happen for a week*, she thought. No, she must be seeing things; everyone was acting normal. Looking around again, it was as if a light had been flicked. They panicked, watching the building collapse, feeling the ground shake. Screams echoed in the air, muted by anxious footsteps. Bodies jostled her, shoving everyone aside. The building toppled, crushing bodies. Her heart pounding, she began to run...

Amina Anwar (13)
High School For Girls, Gloucester

Nobody Else Was There...

Flames everywhere. I stumbled across the wreckage. Nobody else was to be seen.
"Hello?" I called, scared and alone.

No answer. Grass that was once green was now black and burnt. Trees that were once tall were now crumbled logs. The once-beautiful Earth was now a wasteland of destruction. All my family, all my friends, were now gone. I felt miserable and hopeless. I trod past burning bushes underneath a raw, red sky. Suddenly, I came to an incredibly steep cliff. Heart pounding, I looked over the edge. Flames were burning the landscape below; nobody was to be seen...

Rosie Mason (11)
High School For Girls, Gloucester

The Disaster

An outrageous earthquake hit the Caribbean. All the buildings had crumbled and shattered to pieces. The clouds began to get gloomy and they got closer. The world felt like it was spinning. I ambled around the broken island and realised my family hadn't survived the treacherous disaster. How was I going to survive? I threw my backpack on the floor, hoping to find some essential items. The food I had was insufficient. My cat, Willow, was the only thing I owned.

After about three days, I found myself some berries, however, they were poisonous for Willow... Would my cat survive?

Rishita Kari (13)
High School For Girls, Gloucester

Point Of No Return

We could've chosen to save the Earth all those years ago. We ignored the warnings and surpassed the point of no return. I remember years ago someone telling me, "If we don't fix things, nature will." I remember thinking how much easier it would be if we just let that happen... and then it did.

It started off small, heat extending into December, icicles hanging from houses in June. Then came the droughts, the lava, and finally, the Earth just shattered into fragments. I stand alone, among the bodies littering the ground. The end has come. I cannot stop it.

Imogen Flackett (13)
High School For Girls, Gloucester

Cyber Attack

Victoria Sugar was typing away on her laptop when she heard a crash. She looked around but everything was fine. What had happened? Turning her attention back on the laptop, she found that everything was slow. Victoria went to her window and looked outside. Nothing. She looked out again and again.

"Arghh! Arghh!"

Victoria, a spoilt girl, was the most confused she had ever been. Suddenly, she began hearing noises.

"Help! Help!"

There were crashes, bangs and thuds before she heard the four ghostly words, "The network is down..."

Sofia Wolczuk (12)
High School For Girls, Gloucester

The Divine Seas' Wrath

"Beings of Terra!"

A woman had decided to ruin a day of halcyon.

"I am here to put an end to this, and create a new beginning for all!"

Cries filled the tense air. A brave girl stood up.

"What if we don't let you?"

The woman laughed, "My lady, The Queen of Heaven, decreed it, so it shall be."

A wave of black and blue rose to cover the once maya-blue skies, ready to devour the world.

"Remember your executor, Cinta of the Divine Seas."

The shining world was washed away in darkness.

Sophie Gwyneth Isabell Green (12)

High School For Girls, Gloucester

The End Of The World

"This is a story that will soon unfold of death, destruction and the end of the world," came a voice.

I could see the guns, now up ahead in that tranquil, starry sky. Getting closer hour by hour. We'd gone too far this time. I could see people fleeing desperately from their houses and into the night.

"Why?" I asked myself.

I was just an ordinary girl, surrounded by ordinary people. Yet these ordinary people were causing chaos.

There it was, the moment I most remember... And on that day in 2045, everyone was dead, but I survived.

Annette Farrimond (12)
High School For Girls, Gloucester

Thr33

The words were dancing off the page. Three minutes without air, three days without water, three weeks without food.
Suddenly, the world started to turn, spinning even. I scurried outside and darted up into my treehouse. The world flushed by, it started to pour in, gushing past my treehouse. My dad, mum and sister were sure to be dead. My man's best friend was struggling, and soon he sank. My life split in two. As they say, three minutes without air, three days without water and three weeks without food. My memories floated by, flushed away forever and ever.

Katie Jones (12)
High School For Girls, Gloucester

The Final Annihilation

A pair of glowing eyes seemed to bore deep into my entire being. It was then, that I realised how one being could possibly end the world. My teeth bit down on the inside of my lip with such force, that the horrid taste of blood ran onto my tongue. "Scared?"

The creature didn't speak, instead, its words formed like a jigsaw in my mind.

"I have swept away your empires in a single breath, you will be no different."

Dread pooled in my stomach, but conviction quickly smothered it and steeled my gaze. I had to save my world.

Leigh Phillips (15)
High School For Girls, Gloucester

Ravishing To Rot...

Dear Diary,

What is happening on this good old green Earth? Well, I wouldn't call it good... it's more like infected, dead, creepy and dangerous, you get the point. Ever since this so-called pleasant planet was infected, I don't know what to do. I usually depend on my powerful parents, but now they are crazy psychopaths. They *all* are, every single person in my country, and it's all down to the plague. Soon, I know that it will spread across to more countries, unless we stop it somehow, someday. There is just one slight problem...

Damilola Popoola (11)
High School For Girls, Gloucester

What There Used To Be

Guns fired. Souls screamed. Terror and anxiety drowned Ellie's sanity. Bullets flew overhead in the same places birds used to fly. The ground was soaked in glass and acidic puddles where grass and rain used to lie. Around her, fearful shrieks filled the air, not the hustle of the city life.

In the distance, Ellie wept to see piles of soulless victims where the London Eye once stood. Cries of sorrow were drowning out what used to be joyful laughter. With a tear on her cheek, she thought about what London used to be. No firing guns. No screaming souls.

Cassie Freya Barker (12)
High School For Girls, Gloucester

It's Just A Jellyfish...

"Help!"
The sea was swallowing me with its mighty waves.
"I'm coming!"
My friend, Taylor, had finally seen me. She was throwing a rope out, it was my safety line. I reached to grab it, but a jellyfish wrapped its trembling body around me, sending an electric wave through my body. I slipped from my surfboard, the only thing saving me from drowning. My arm was screaming with pain as I sank to the seabed. I could feel the steady movement of the sand on my back. There was no way I could survive this time. This was the end.

Jasmine Richards (12)
High School For Girls, Gloucester

The Volcano

I was perched on the boulders surrounding our magnificent volcano that would sleep forever, basking in the golden rays of the sun. Closing my eyes, I allowed my mind to drift to this morning's news report. They said that the volcano would erupt again soon and it would be the first time in a thousand years. I didn't believe a word.
Suddenly, the volcano unleashed a tumultuous growl, as if it was yearning to release the pressure inside. Smoke began billowing from the top. I covered my mouth and ran as if my life depended on it. Because it did...

Natasha Doherty (12)
High School For Girls, Gloucester

The Red Race

A red fiery liquid was spewing over the ancient, disintegrated volcano. The liquid slithered down the rocky terrain, like a snake following its prey. Rocks tumbled from the pressure. This volcano had been inactive for over one hundred years. Instinct kicked in and I turned sharply and began running. I ran as quickly as my legs would let me, but I could still hear the nearby screams of civilians. Fear started to spread around my body, but I had to stay calm. Reluctantly, I turned my head and saw the horror that had just occurred. This surely was the end...

Nara Ellen Cox-Sonora (13)
High School For Girls, Gloucester

Water Lost

Sarah peered out from her shelter cautiously. The devastation from the tsunami (which had only hit hours earlier) lay all around her. Thoughts raced through her head. Was she the only survivor? What happened to Jodie and the others? Was anyone else alive? Sarah slowly edged out of the shelter, climbing over the blackened debris. She looked around the resort, which was demolished. For the first time, she noticed the eerie silence. She could smell the stench of damp wood and taste the salty seawater.

"Over here," whispered a muffled voice.

Molly Buckley (11)
High School For Girls, Gloucester

Bomb Of Life

Crash! It was another bomb, *thirtieth one this week.* As she drew another tally line in her journal, a shiver ran down her spine. She put on her now dirty, ragged, grey coat which gave her a slight burst of warmth, like a spark of fire. She looked at her wallet - just two tuppences left. Only if she was as rich as she was cold... Now *that* would be good. She went back to her 'shelter' (well it was more of a ruin). She stepped inside and rubbed her eyes, making sure she wasn't dreaming. She couldn't believe it...

Evelyn Abraham (12)

High School For Girls, Gloucester

Earthquake Finding!

So there I was, standing amongst all the rubble and wreckage, staring into the distance, waiting to find survivors - if there *were* any. My team had been searching for days on end in hope.

"Boss! We've found one!" called Joe.

I rushed over, grabbed his collar and screamed, "What? Where?"

In shock, all he could do was point. I sprinted over to my team and dropped to the floor. As I heard the muffled cries, I pushed the bricks aside and pulled out a young man. He turned to face me and I saw him. My brother!

Brooke Richardson (12)
High School For Girls, Gloucester

The Gun

He hid. Scared and anxious. *Bang!* Was this a childish joke? Sam didn't know what to do. Hours passed... The shooter was outside his classroom, and his parents wouldn't answer their phone. A book, a chair, a table were all he had. *Bang!* The shooter was getting nearer to his class. He and his friends huddled together. Bravery was no longer alive. Tension flooded the room, he could feel it. The protection gun was on the other side of the room. The door creaked open... *Bang!* Was Sam dead? Did he survive the horror?

Isabella Macaraeg (12)
High School For Girls, Gloucester

The Day That Changed London

The sun beamed down on the city of London. Samuel Pepys was in his study, letting his pen dance across the pages whilst listening to the birds sing. Then came silence and the hairs on the back of his neck stood up. Blood-curdling screams rang around the city. Sweat trickled down his forehead and into his wig. Samuel edged towards the window, ready to open it, when a terrible sight greeted him. Flames were swallowing the city, engulfing everything in its path. His city was being destroyed, and there was nothing that he could do... Not now, not ever.

Daisy Meggs (11)
High School For Girls, Gloucester

Animal Kingdom

Duck! thought Zowbi to herself as a piece of metal flew by. It was an elephant who had taken the shot at her. It was beside the king of the Animal Kingdom, King Vendra II, whose big, bushy mane grew out of every direction.

Despite the situation she was in, Zowbi still loved all animals. Her stomach rumbled as she had to fast with the little food in the now collapsed house. Suddenly, Tallulah the monkey let out a piercing scream whilst throwing a piece of wood at Zowbi's head. *Doomf!* Everything went all black and fuzzy.

Alice Fuller (11)
High School For Girls, Gloucester

When Zombies Join Forces With The Elements

Zombies were just brainless, groaning things right? As it turned out, they knew how to tear open petrol cans and send anything up into flames using a lighter. This was exactly what they did. The flames grew... Soon it got to a point where there was nothing that others could do except stand there, gazing at the blazing beasts. As my lungs filled up with their poisoned breath, my body became heavier. The sky started spinning and before I knew it I was lying on the ground. My eyelids fell and my pulse slackened. *Is this how my life ends?*

Niamh Gillies (12)
High School For Girls, Gloucester

The Beginning Of The End

Ever tried running from lava? Wouldn't recommend it. It's hot and impossible. What am I currently doing? The smell of rotten eggs hit my nose, making my eyes water. Sulphur! As I ran, dodging flying rocks, I dug deep into my pockets and pulled out a knife. *Oh, that'll be really helpful when trying to block the sulphur.* I searched the rest of my pockets until at last, I found a handkerchief. I covered my mouth and nose with it. Now my only priority was to find high ground. A huge rock blocked my path. There was no escape...

Evie Griffiths (12)
High School For Girls, Gloucester

The Metal Birds

I froze, gazing out at the destruction around me. Heaps of rubble, stone and wood. Buildings had no walls, roofs, or just simply weren't there. Rotating slowly, I looked for a sign of life. I wanted to know if I was alone. Stumbling forwards, I began to yell. A shadow appeared on the ground, just big enough for me to make it out. They looked like metal birds. I started running, I wanted to put as much distance between me and the creatures as possible. Clutching my torch tightly, I ran towards the nearest house. Then my world shattered...

Alexandra Caroline Stroud (12)
High School For Girls, Gloucester

Bunker 205

Beep! Beep! Beep! Rushing down the stairs, I ran into the vault, locking the door behind me. The bomb wasn't supposed to drop this early. Scanning the chamber, I crept to the controls. Dad had tried to teach me them before he was taken. A red light glowed behind the buttons. My stomach dropped like a brick from a plane. Panic took control. I quickly shot to the air vents, they had always been faulty but I never paid any attention. Thick green smoke was pouring in. I saw a hand reaching towards me, and then my vision went blank.

Eleanor Mitchell (12)
High School For Girls, Gloucester

Crashing Down

Rubble was everywhere. Grasping onto Dodge as tight as possible, I saw the dust start to clear. Dodge looked as scared as me. I glanced around; metal framework stood where my house used to stand. I crouched under it. I daren't move in case it collapsed. I thought my heart was going to burst out of my chest. Dodge whimpered. He was keeping me warm. I heard movement outside and my heart began racing again. I could hear people moving rubble and I began to see light. Dodge ran through the gap and suddenly everything collapsed on top of me.

Olivia Hattersley-Newman (13)
High School For Girls, Gloucester

You Can't Change The Past

The whole Earth shudders.
"We advise you to stay sheltered as much as possible."
The birds, now bullets. The shelters, now a sign of weakness. The friends, now enemies.
The light has faded, and the hope has too. I need my family.
The people are scouring the ground for possessions. Many left their bunkers to save others, yet never came back, and if they did, they were sure to have a shorter life expectancy. I hear a wail in the distance, but there is mainly silence. People stare. Hoping for things to change.

Niamh Eleanor Beard (12)
High School For Girls, Gloucester

Sophie's Race For Life

"Help, help!" screamed Sophie and her family as they fled from their home right at the foot of Mount Fuji, Honshu, Japan.
They ran as fast as a bullet, trying to escape from the orange heat that is lava, which was quickly chasing them down the mountain. Sophie fell, but quickly got back up again and kept going. She was so tired and started struggling to breathe, due to the amount of energy she was using. Sophie was not sure whether she could keep going for much longer, but she knew she *had* to. Would she make it?

Isobel Watt (11)
High School For Girls, Gloucester

Fanfare Of Death For The Common Man

Cycling back from music rehearsal, his trumpet bouncing on his back, Reggie was soaked from the rain. He could still hear the sound of cymbals crashing away in the distance, or was it the wind? As he looked ahead, the glowing comfort and safety of his own home encouraged him to keep going.

Later, reports of the shocking devastation had surfaced, but most poignant of all was the last camera shot of a young man disappearing beneath the waves, his trumpet held afloat. Reggie had used his last breath of air to play his final note...

Archisha Pant (13)

High School For Girls, Gloucester

Lost And Found

My dad owns NASA. Me and my mother are on Mars, searching for my missing brother, Tim. He was last seen here. I stop and tuck away the necklace he bought me. We wander around until Mars rumbles; an earthquake separates me from Mum. I cry for help, watching her fall. *Not her too!* I've lost my mum and my brother. I slip and catch a grip on the edge. I feel like I'm on the monkey bars at primary school. Further away, "Tierra!" echoes. I am then being hauled up by my necklace and, to my surprise, it's Tim.

Alisha Shaikh (12)
High School For Girls, Gloucester

Disaster On Horseback

I was cantering around the arena on Ollie, my horse, when I sensed something was wrong. There was a peculiar feeling in the air. Ollie was acting unusually, he wasn't responding to my actions and was moving slower than usual. I pulled to a halt and dismounted before leading him to his stable. I tied him up and phoned my mum, but she didn't pick up. I phoned my dad, and he didn't either. My instincts kicked in, this was an earthquake. I put on my coat and prepared for the worst.
"Stay calm," I told myself.

Amy Larkman (12)
High School For Girls, Gloucester

The Only Survivor

I woke up suddenly, my sheets drenched in sweat. The drought had been going on for weeks now. There was less food and water. I got out of bed and quietly tiptoed downstairs so I didn't wake anyone. I sat down and watched TV with a bowl of cornflakes.

An hour later, and still nobody had come downstairs; nobody had ever slept in for this long. I turned the TV off and tiptoed back upstairs to my parents' room. They were nowhere to be seen, and neither were my sisters. Everyone I knew was gone... Was I the only survivor?

Imogen Goodwin (12)
High School For Girls, Gloucester

Alone

I still remember the scream that cut through the silence. The sign that everything was going to change. I feel sweat dripping down the back of my neck and I recognise that familiar metallic taste in my mouth. I must keep moving. I don't really know why, but it was the last thing my father told me. "Run!"

As soon as those words parted from his lips, my family were killed. I saw my home amongst the rubble. I was terrified. As I ran through town, everything I saw was chaos, and that brought me here, alone.

Amy Gettings (12)
High School For Girls, Gloucester

Fire

Ashes, nothing but ashes. Her house was gone. Her parents were gone. Everything was gone. Suddenly she realised that the barren land was the least of her problems. Being the last person left on Earth, her natural instinct was to cry for help. Her tears drowned her face. Her faint voice calling out for help, she could hear a series of cries of help following on from her. Praise the Lord, someone was still alive! She ran in the direction of the cries. Thirsty, hungry and tired, but she had to carry on if she wanted to survive.

Khushi Saini (13)
High School For Girls, Gloucester

The Call Of The Siren

It was acting as a siren, beautiful yet pulling me closer with every passing second. There was no escape, and it was crawling up my body, rapidly showing me no mercy. The dark liquid, too thick to be water and the colour was indescribable. By now it was swirling menacingly around my waist. I cried out for help but it was futile, there was no one; I was alone. My one fear had come true. Tears streamed down my face as I wished for the soft, warm embrace of my mother. The world went black, everything I knew had faded.

Kira Wendy Holmes (13)
High School For Girls, Gloucester

The End

I look around and pause to see what my world has become. Wasteland with nothing to call home, I mistakenly breathe in the sulphate-contaminated air. I am suffocating, the air is like a dagger of fire, stabbing me in the lungs. A dagger which I can't escape from. I tremble in fear as another piece of scolding magma shoots out of a lava-filled hole. Nobody knows the cause of this catastrophe, only that this will initiate the end of the world. I am one of the last survivors, but right now, I wish I wasn't...

Eleanor Margaret Harbottle (11)
High School For Girls, Gloucester

Emily And The Great Flood!

Once upon a time, there was a little girl named Emily. She had a dog named Brownie. Today was the most horrendous day ever. There was a flood. As Emily got out of her bed, she noticed that her shoes were drenched in water. She ran to her windowsill and could hear sirens and rescue boats covering Gloucester. She packed her things and yelled for her dog to come upstairs to her bedroom. There was no reply. She called again but there was no reply. Just then, she heard her dog barking for help. What should she do?

Alicia George (11)
High School For Girls, Gloucester

The Fire Creature

Stephanie grimaced. She sat up and spat out a tooth that had fallen out when a loose branch fell out and hit her in the face. They had been running through the forest. Fire was chasing after them, a hungry creature with intent to catch its prey. She looked over at Eve who was covered in dirt and burns. Stephanie tried to clear her mind of the image of her best friend, Riley, being engulfed by the flames. They had been so close, but now they were so far away. The deadly wildfire stole her life.

Adele Sawyer (11)
High School For Girls, Gloucester

A Living Nightmare!

The lights all turned off and I sat in the corner with Mum. Trembling in fear, my eyes started to sting and my nose made a sniffling noise. Mum comforted me. Then the floor started to rumble. I felt Mum hug me tighter. My eyes began to flood with tears and spill over my burning cheeks. The walls started to shake, and out the window, I saw a flash of lightning. Me and Mum started to panic. I could hear screams from other houses.

"Don't panic," Mum whispered, and then the house tilted...

Anjum Rai (11)
High School For Girls, Gloucester

After The Bang

I wake up staring into the barrel of a gun. I don't know how I got here, I can't remember a thing. I look around at the wasteland surrounding me. *Bang!* I see myself on the floor with blood spewing out of my body. I suppose this is what it's like to be dead. Then something comes towards my body, it gouges at my flesh. I start yelling and shrieking as it plunges its sharp, blade-like teeth into my pale corpse. It doesn't seem to hear me. I don't know what this creature is...

Emma Milne (12)
High School For Girls, Gloucester

Tsunami Surprise

No one expected to see a ten-foot wave today. Screams shattered my ears as I raced around the classroom, looking for my belongings. The teachers were yelling down my throat to get me outside. However, I am Moanna, I do not go down that easily. Backpack securely on, I struggled up towards the ceiling of the flooded room, my lung capacity stretching as water entered my mouth. Finally, fresh air. I knew too well that my classmates were going to die down there. I trembled with fear, and the next wave hit.

Madeleine Spinner (12)
High School For Girls, Gloucester

Make-Up Guru Overboard

My arms flailed as water swirled above my head. My lungs heaved as I clambered onto the bed. Debris thrashed at the mattress and I shuddered. If only the sea hadn't swept my hoodie away. My acrylic nails were mangled and I wish that I had worn waterproof mascara. My mind wandered back to the blaring sirens of the ship. My brother panicked as I forced him aside, determined to save my fake tan. Frosty water licked at my feet, I was sinking. Again, my arms flailed as water swirled above my head...

Chloe Smith (12)
High School For Girls, Gloucester

Dreams And Bombs

I just woke up. I had that dream again. I couldn't get it out of my head. It controlled everyday activities and kept me up at night. It described the world worse than it already was. The atomic bomb expected to soon hit the area had struck, spreading its toxicity in the form of a mushroom cloud. People had been travelling north for ages, trying to escape its wrath. However, some didn't travel far enough. It woke me up. Alone in my cell-like room, deep in the bunker, it left me scared.

Gracie McTaggart-Spiers (11)
High School For Girls, Gloucester

The Murderous Eden

The lush greenery is taking over bit by bit. I am now surrounded by it everywhere, it looks like a bouquet full of flowers spilling out ubiquitously. It seems beautiful at first glance, drawing you in. However, at night, they twist and climb, catching their prey. Gradually, someone you know, a family member or a friend, is gone. In the night, I can feel them entwining around me, squeezing me tight until I fall into their clutches. No more Camellia Beaumont, only sixteen, dead and forgotten.

Sophia Dumbelton (11)
High School For Girls, Gloucester

It's Cold Out There

It was the twenty-first of July, and the whole world had gone black. My pet cat had died and I was all alone. I wanted to visit my family, but after all the pain I'd caused, I knew I couldn't do it.

Days had passed, and it was now August. The cold breeze wrapped around the town like a blanket. People were passing out instantly. I had to visit my mum, but when I entered the house, it was too late. She was already dead. I was now all alone until my time would eventually come...

Meerab Tahir (12)
High School For Girls, Gloucester

The Last Fire

My eyes blazed with the fire that my spiteful dad created. I knew this wasn't my wild imagination, it was real. I ran as fast as I could away from the suffocating smoke. I ran until I came to a forest. The path I was following stopped right in front of me. A labyrinth of trees seemed to whisper and mock me. Where should I go? I saw that the insane fire had me cornered, what should I do? I knew that I'd die no matter what path I took. I opened my water bottle and took my last sip.

Malindi Maughan (11)
High School For Girls, Gloucester

The Day My Family Died

The water had already engulfed most of the house. All I had now was my life. When I looked into the murky water, which had taken the lives of my family, all I saw was my contorted reflection. The lonely reflection of a young girl who had lost everything. The only thing she had left were the memories. A tear slid down my emotionless face, my cries broke the eerie silence. I lost myself in the house that I used to call home, which was now keeping me as a prisoner.

Olivia Hopwood (13)
High School For Girls, Gloucester

Flooding Catastrophe

Dear Kylie,

Here I am stuck in this dreadful flood, I don't know how I am going to get out of here! My sister (who was only four years old) has sadly been dragged away by the tremendous beast. I don't know how I will survive, my family are doing the best they can to get us out of here. I think this is going to be the last day I can talk to you. For this very moment I just want to say thank you for being there for me every step of the way...

Diana Philip (11)
High School For Girls, Gloucester

The Earth's Revenge

The world is annoyed. We've been treating it like rubbish. So it's come to get us instead. We are disappearing like ghosts from a misty past. Family by family, building by building. Each death leaves an empty space on Earth. You see, the world is eradicating us. Swallowing us up like popcorn. Oh no! The world is opening, it is black...

Ana Navarro-Garcia (11)
High School For Girls, Gloucester

There Was No Warning

They had come without warning, without reason, but they knew what they wanted and what they wanted was us.

I am running; my legs are burning, my head is pounding and my breath is coming in ever shorter rasps. But I can't stop, they can't catch me because I know what they did to the others, to my family. I'd heard the screams and saw the bodies. They are gaining on me now, their bodies more suited to the pursuit of prey. I stumble, don't fall, but it's too late. A skeletal hand grasps my shoulder and everything goes dark.

Bertie Parkes (12)
Rendcomb College School, Rendcomb

Plague

The clouds of smoke and sand filled my lungs. Buildings fell into a heap of bricks and flames. I sat trembling, feeling sweat gather up on my brow. Sand and fire had filled the market square. The flames raged with fury, with intent to burn. The plague would soon be here; it followed the heat, it grew stronger and became even more life-threatening after every town it went through. Would I catch it? You never know. The longer I sat and watched, the bigger the chance. In time, I would leave this city. I longed for answers.

Henry Carr (12)
Rendcomb College School, Rendcomb

The Burn

Sweat dripped down my nose, burns formed on my pale skin. Everybody was gone, dead on the floor. They all had a temperature of above fifty degrees. I struggled to breathe, all the oxygen was going. I struggled to walk. It felt like everything I touched was a radiator. I crawled along the ground towards a pool. I fell in but it was warm, very warm. However, it was still cooler than the air. I turned around and there was a man through the ripples, wearing black. I could see he was holding a gun. I thought it was over...

Thomas Henry George (13)
Rendcomb College School, Rendcomb

They're Coming

It was an evening with a blood-red sky. I saw them in the sky falling endlessly. They were burning a bright light. I noticed my family scrambling towards the shelter. I had to join them, but I didn't want to. The bombs were falling quickly, my family were begging me to stay. I walked towards them, closed the shelter door. I went to face the bombs as they struck a white cloud of explosions. The smoke engulfed me. Something strange started building inside of me, filling me up. Then suddenly... *pop!*

Edward Sweeney (13)
Rendcomb College School, Rendcomb

Not Again

I woke up to see the white ceiling with a bright light shining into my eyes, blinding me. As the beeping of machines and the screams of babies down the hallway filled my ears, I sat up, wondering where I was. My memories started to flow back to me. I heard a rumbling sound in the distance. It was extremely loud, followed by screams. Then it all stopped. I finally realised where I was. A hospital. As the rumbling got louder and louder, cracks began to appear on the walls of my room.

Chloe Witt (13)
Rendcomb College School, Rendcomb

Before It Rang

Wind swept through the fallen leaves, the trees whistled cries in agony. They fought their way to the entrance, their auburn hair resembling the mane of a lion. They gazed around the room in astonishment, children scattering the room, screaming and giggling, running around the classroom. They longingly peered out the window, wishing they were elsewhere. The trees stopped whistling, birds retreated out of sight. Clouds smeared the skies. Suddenly, the floor grumbled. Lights overhead swung. Darkness smothered the room. Windows shattered. Everyone scrambled under their desks. Water seeped in. They clutched onto their brave table leg.

Lara Mueller (15)
Wyedean School, Sedbury

Tsar

"There's only one word I remember before it dropped. 'Peace'. The war lasted just seven hours. Ending with a Tsar, an explosion bigger than what was once Mount Everest. Radiation deadlier than the Seven Seas combined. It covered the land like a thin blanket. My village wasn't affected by the explosion, due to our wall of dense forest. But... The horrors to follow were what killed us, what killed us off. That's where I messed up. I went out of the sanctuary and I... sorry. I was poisoned," he sniffed. "If you find this, remember the number 2318. Please." *Static.*

Seán Hart (15)
Wyedean School, Sedbury

Stranded

"What? How? When? Why am I on this island? I don't deserve this!"
Ashleigh was stranded on an island, with nothing around her.
"I didn't do anything wrong."
Ashleigh only had a fishing rod and a fishing net.
"Where are my clothes? Where is the food?"
There was nothing. As she was thinking about how unfair her life was, all of a sudden night dawned upon her. She got tired and went to sleep. There were dangerous creatures in the sea that she didn't know about. Ashleigh awoke in the middle of the night to a sound, then suddenly... *gulp!*

Shannyn Hoare (12)
Wyedean School, Sedbury

Life Or Death?

Penelope was trapped between life and death.
Everyone was screaming, "Stay inside!"
No one actually knew what was going on.
Suddenly, the ceiling fell, it fell on Penelope's leg.
She was screaming and crying for help, but she
was trapped, alone, cold and hungry. All of a
sudden, Jasmine, Penelope's bestie, came running
in.
"Jasmine, help I'm stuck!" screamed Penelope.
There was a loud bang and the building started to
collapse, they were stuck. It was dark and there
was smoke.
"We need to get out!" they screamed.
But they were trapped!

Lourdes Mann (12)
Wyedean School, Sedbury

Torn

I've lost all sense of time. It might've been days, weeks since it happened, but my mind is a mirror. I can't stop reflecting on the horrors I've seen. My soul's a chamber for the screams of those now silent. I remember my world tearing, quivering and cracking. Buildings falling and hitting the ground, like a piece of glass shattering into millions of splinters. I was trapped. Vast wounds opened the Earth. Death glowered menacingly. I couldn't escape this wild, stormy attack. Then the guns stopped firing. The battle was over. Without hope, I was torn, just like my world.

Gabriella Watkins (11)
Wyedean School, Sedbury

My Boiling Point

I wake up, my heart weaker and slower than before. I stumble outside, it's even hotter, I can't cope much longer. It's been two years since I last felt a cool breeze! There are lifeless bodies around me, I cough and splutter in the unbearable heat. I can't help it. The amount of dead humanity is outrageous. All I and many other people are wishing for is rain. Just one drip can keep me alive! Suddenly, villagers shout, "There is water!"
We run to the well; there is nothing there! I cough. This is it, it's over, *I'm* over... *Drip...*

Faye Martin (11)
Wyedean School, Sedbury

The Final Days!

Days before it happened, there were noises of eruptions. This carried on for days. David and his sister, Samantha, decided to flee. A short time after they left the once inactive volcano, it had begun erupting golden lava on to the village called Caldicot. They lived in a country called Magor. The volcano was Mount Etna, known for being the world's worst volcano.

After they reached safety, they realised they were the luckiest people in the world.

Later that same day, they found out that their home had been destroyed. They were safe. Samantha and David had successfully escaped.

Megan Lilly Sweet (12)
Wyedean School, Sedbury

Olympus Mons - An Interstellar Voyage

With a hiss of escaping air, the hatch opened and Luna exited the shuttle via it. Then she saw the glorious, crimson landscape, barren except for rocks. Then, helpless, before she could do anything, Luna heard a faint rumble and directly behind her, the scarlet sand burst open and a khaki substance came forth. It poured out like a fountain, pulverising the rocks. Luna's ship did not stand a chance, it too vapourised within seconds, the liquid eating away at it.

Suddenly, a beeping noise woke Luna from her daze. It was her warning bracelet saying: 'Incoming solar winds'.

Idris McKie (12)
Wyedean School, Sedbury

Technology

"Help!" she screamed. "Help!"

But no one came. Pitch-black, Ava sat in the dark, then a light flickered. The door opened and a person appeared all in black.

They had a deep voice and said, "Ava, come with me."

As she walked, she felt like the floor was breaking beneath her feet. She wondered what the year was, she asked the man and he said, "2069."

She replied, "Really? It's been fifty years, how?"

He said, "People have somehow invented technology, and you have been revived for a special reason..."

Emily Grace Burke (13)
Wyedean School, Sedbury

Why Me?

Why me? All alone on this empty island. I know after the massive earthquake, everyone got evacuated to islands but why has the government left me all alone on this island? I'm only fourteen. *Snap!* What was that? It's only me here. *Snap!* It's getting closer, it might be the government to take me to a different island.
"Yes! Over here!"
I can see them, wait... That's not the government. They're not even people, they are massive! What *are* they? This island is uninhabited. No, it can't be... They can't be. Why here?

Alice Morgan (12)
Wyedean School, Sedbury

Terror In Tenerife!

It was a scorching hot morning in Tenerife when Fleur and Rosanna were in the pool. Fleur's parents had just nipped out to the local shops. After a few hours, Fleur thought it was weird how her parents hadn't returned. So she went to call her mum, then she noticed she had numerous missed calls. She immediately called her mum back.

Her mum said, "Don't worry about me and your father, get you and your sister to safety."

"Why?" asked Fleur.

There was an eerie silence.

"Hello?" said Fleur, but there was no one there...

Georgia Watkin-Jones (12)
Wyedean School, Sedbury

The Final Days

After the volcano erupted, everyone came back to Pompeii. Megan was the only one with hope. Everyone else was so disappointed, they'd lost everything! They were all so depressed. Megan wanted to rebuild everything but no one was up to it. She tried rebuilding the city all by herself, but she failed every time. Everyone laughed at her until they realised that they wouldn't have homes to live in. Suddenly, when everyone stopped laughing, they realised they had to help Megan rebuild the city. It took a while but when they were finished, everyone had a beautiful new home.

Samantha Grace Williamson (11)
Wyedean School, Sedbury

The Thing

The wind echoed through the town, an eerie silence drifted through the area. Teenagers were met by this. No one knew what was happening. It was every man for themselves. A blood-curdling scream surprised the teenagers. The friends, Charlie and Cali, didn't know if it was a man or a beast. Charlie took his phone out and saw that he had a voicemail. He pressed play; what he heard was catastrophic.

"Charlie, son, if you get this... Your life is in danger. Love you, son, stay safe. We can't help you now, but you have still got a chance. Arghh!"

Carys Martin (12)
Wyedean School, Sedbury

Falling

Search helicopters flew above, teasing me. As the building toppled down, my heart began beating faster. I was about to die. *Boom.*

"Why aren't I dead?" I wondered.

Feebly, I tried to breathe. My lungs burned. Ash coated my surroundings like dark snow. It was then that I saw it. A body lay face down, a few metres away. I crawled over, praying. I rolled the body over, I wanted to scream. A familiar face stared up at me, death in her eyes. My mother. My mother was dead.

"No, no!" I whispered. "No."

Isabelle Walker (11)
Wyedean School, Sedbury

Ghost Town

I look around. This city burned to rubble. I can make out where the munitions factory was. That was where it all ended. They were making a massive nuke for the renowned president Ronald Bump. It was the hottest day of the whole year. The nuke exploded. Whole cities were wiped out, but I'm still here staring at a barren ghost town. My family were wiped out; I'm the only one remaining. There are still bodies here, somewhere in the rubble. Possessions left on the ground. I can still feel the chemicals in the air. Wait, the rubble just moved...

Archie Underwood (11)
Wyedean School, Sedbury

Another World

My clenched fists hung, glazed with blood. I stood, not interfering with the catastrophe soon to occur. I made that mistake before, in the other dimension. The light pranced from the elevated point, which protruded from a luminous, pentagon-shaped building. Suddenly the glass shattered, revealing a dozen armed soldiers in black uniforms. They began charging at us. I saw behind them a wind demolishing these cruel killers. I had no weapon but I had fists. I took a swipe, then another, and then a third. My hand plummeted through the black portal...

James Hardinge (11)
Wyedean School, Sedbury

Fire City

Scorched like fire, a deep red burn spread over my left leg, embroidering it. The ruby sky had burgundy clouds, twisting and turning. It was Hell, Hell had come. The ginormous face of the Devil covered half of the red sky. It had filthy, yellow pointed horns and red scales for skin. It had a sickening, evil smile. I was frozen, staring up at the horrid face. Thinking drastically about what to do, I lifted up a ten-storey skyscraper that had come crashing down. Satan used his mind to send buildings to smash down to the floor. Fire was everywhere.

Harry Graham (11)
Wyedean School, Sedbury

Silence

It's dark. We were having so much fun dancing in the streets when the ground started shaking. An earthquake. I didn't even know it could happen in Chepstow, but it did. I don't know where Elliot is. I can hear him, but not see him. Norah's dead, she won't reply. All I can smell is dust, blood and death. All I can hear are people crying out in pain and buildings falling, which tells me the earthquake is not over. Then silence. Somehow, the silence is deafening. It feels like the world has gone. Sometimes silence is violent.

Chloe Susan Dolan (12)
Wyedean School, Sedbury

Washed Away

The weather had been terrible, with heavy rain falling for several days. My faithful Jeep had always felt so safe. Suddenly, there was water rising over the bonnet. I was caught in the middle of deep flood water from the surrounding fields. The volume of the torrent lifted the Jeep into the air. Panic surged through me as I battled to gain control of the vehicle. I knew I needed to get out but couldn't open the door. The icy cold water was powerful, and the Jeep soon began to capsize. Gasping for breath, my head just above the water...

Ethan Joseph Wood (12)
Wyedean School, Sedbury

The Flood

The siren went off. There was a tsunami coming. There was a rush to get to a high place, and quickly. The people were running for their lives, I could see the tsunami coming and once it curled, everyone who was on the ground was doomed. The people were thrown around by the strength of the waves. Then the trees were uprooted, tossed around, and waves then hit buildings. Those that were fragile crumbled like matchsticks. Those that saw the tsunami coming were able to reach very high ground. These people survived, but they were devastated.

Jack Newman (11)
Wyedean School, Sedbury

The Very End

The eruptions had finished and the air was thick with soot. I couldn't see anyone who was still alive. I gulped, knowing this was the end. Fire crackled around me. I froze in fear. The air was getting thicker, it was like hell. I climbed to the nearest building, but the eruptions had started again. I dived behind a car as molten rocks landed. I thought everyone was dead, but I could hear screaming around me. Was someone coming to save us? I watched a rock fly towards me, it hit me and the pain was unbearable. Everything went black.

Charlie Howells (12)
Wyedean School, Sedbury

World Of Undead

A zombie apocalypse had struck, there were only a few survivors and Sam was one of them. He was a sixteen-year-old boy. His parents had been killed and turned into zombies. Sam was surviving with his two friends, Will and Joe. The two teenagers were very brave and they claimed they were not scared of anything. The three of them ventured out, hoping to find more civilians. Sam, Will and Joe were walking through the infected city until they walked up to a herd of zombies. The group of boys didn't know what to do. They decided to run.

Sam Cantle (11)
Wyedean School, Sedbury

Lava Run

Years ago, disaster struck. All we could do was run. The volcano erupted and many died. The lava looked like melted gold. We ran into the sea. Children cried and could smell the foul stench of smoke emitting from the lava. As the lava was coming towards us, I could feel that horrid heat. Many died from exhaustion. We swam around the island, but it was submerged in lava. It was burning. All we could do was live in the shallow parts of the island shore.

Years later we have evolved into something not human. We are unknown aquatics.

Caitlin Paige Firmin (11)

Wyedean School, Sedbury

The Eruption

I live on a small volcanic island. It is beautiful, we are surrounded by crystal-clear waters.

I want to take you back to last year though, when the island was nearly no more. Our volcano, Mount Bus, last erupted seventy years ago. On the nineteenth of July, there was a distinct smell in the air. Smoke appeared, and visibility was not good. Spouts of rock began to shoot up into the sky, reaching incredible heights. Lava spewed its way down the mountainside. It was time to evacuate. I had to move quickly and gather my belongings.

Lucas Bowen (12)
Wyedean School, Sedbury

The Eruption

As I looked around the town I was born in, I realised the temperature was rising slowly. As I live by a volcano, this wasn't a big deal, until I looked up at the volcano and there I saw a massive cloud of smoke.

I screamed, "Mum, Dad, come quickly!"

Suddenly, a large amount of scalding hot lava shot out of the volcano. I knew that our lives would be in terrible danger if we stayed there, so I packed my penknife, some rope, food, water, my phone, phone charger, a tent, sleeping bag and clothes. Then I set off.

Georgia Huson (12)
Wyedean School, Sedbury

The World Ending

"Breaking news, a meteor has crashed on Earth, we advise everyone to clear the city, for safety. Thank you, we will update you soon."
Oh, by the way, I'm Mike, I'm an explorer, so I am the only one left in the city and I am looking for the meteor. Lots of my friends and family have seen it, but they died when they got back. They said that there is a clock in the meteor and currently it is in Trafalgar Square. There it is, the meteor. And there it is, the clock. I'm going to touch it. *3...2...1...*

Devon Powell (12)
Wyedean School, Sedbury

Silence

It had been years since it started. Nearly all of humanity is extinct. Nobody knew what it was from the first death to the last death. We know what is it now, it's a virus that spreads very fast. People have nearly made a cure for it, but there's a problem, all the doctors are dead. The virus is getting stronger, at this very minute. Now everyone is nearly dead, people try to move to different countries but they just spread it more. There are not many people left, there's not much time. Only the strongest will survive.

Ioan Day (11)
Wyedean School, Sedbury

Stay Or Run

It all started in Thailand, 2004. The biggest tsunami struck but that was the first one there ever was.

One year later there was another big one. It went five thousand miles an hour, crushing the world where it stood. I could hear it knocking down buildings, I could see it knocking down everything I saw. I could taste the blood from the dead. When I touched the water, death appeared and I could smell death coming as it crushed past. It was the end, it would hunt down everyone forever until the world died. Try to survive.

Charlie Peter Steven Bethell (11)
Wyedean School, Sedbury

Escaped Rhino

There was a rhino, but it wasn't a normal rhino. This rhino had a magic horn that killed people. He lived in a zoo and was extremely powerful. He was hard to tame until one day something happened. The rhino escaped and everyone was worrying as he could kill people, he was going everywhere and ruining everything. Rory the rhino killed many people, so everyone had to hide so they wouldn't be killed. However, he managed to kill lots of people.

After that, Rory got caught and taken away and then got put down.

Caitlin Jennings (13)
Wyedean School, Sedbury

We Are Going On A Bear Hunt

My best friends and I went to Alaska with school last year, and we found ourselves lost in a white wonderland desert. Izzy thought it would be fun to go hide in the fluffy, cloud-like snow. But, she made such a horrendous sound that she woke up a suspiciously rare bear. You're probably wondering why it was so rare. Even Amber didn't know what it was. It had royal-blue fur, with streaks of hot pink. We told the locals about this mysterious animal, and they just all looked at each other and screamed fearfully.

Jasmine Fellows (11)
Wyedean School, Sedbury

Water

I was sat in a normal English class when I heard a rumbling sound. Our teacher checked outside the class, and shouted out, "Run!" Everyone got out their seat and started running. Still, I had no idea what was going on. I looked back, my best friend was sat in the corner, crying. I ran towards her. We both ran out the class. I looked sidewards, still I saw nothing. The sound got louder, it was catching up to me. I heard all the voices crying out as children ran from all directions. Then I saw the water...

Amber Morgan (11)
Wyedean School, Sedbury

World At War

We locked eyes as our noses twitched. A now unfamiliar aroma had drifted into our shelter. We didn't even consult each other. We knew we had to follow it. All I could think about was the years gone by since this war had ruined everything. The smell reminded me of the luxuries we used to have. This aroma had picked up our lifeless bodies and was forcefully pulling us out of our comfort. We got closer. The metal door opened. It was a lure. A wall of brown shirts awaited us. All we could do was kneel before them.

Alex Bint (15)
Wyedean School, Sedbury

Fallen Sun

My legs were trembling. The wall which had once stood in front of me had now disappeared. Like a blade of grass, I stood alone, not knowing if anything was out there. I knew the sun had fallen! On the horizon, the sun shone brightly, patches of fire surrounded me. I kept silent, still too shocked to speak. That was when I saw it, the shadow in the distance. It was a human's shadow. They turned around, but it realised there was something different about them. Suddenly, it hit me. This person was not a person...

Hannah Gibson (12)
Wyedean School, Sedbury

A Volcanic Catastrophe

A loud rumbling fills the air. Slow pus-like lava creeps from a volcano. The sky is a painful orange. Smoke erupts with a strong force.

"Run!" my mother shouts.

I grab my gigantic bag and scream goodbye through the mist, whilst Snowflake, my horse, gallops off into the gloom. A warm fire on a tall, majestic, mountainous area reminds me of home. Tears like hailstones run down my cheeks. Suddenly, an explosion of lava. I am flown backwards, through the mist away from my home, far away forever.

Florence Lily Hills (11)
Wyedean School, Sedbury

The World's Biggest Disaster!

I looked out of the window and meteoroids started falling. We almost got hit by one. Suddenly, we started losing oxygen. Our oxygen was now very low, like thirty more breaths and all of us might be dead. Ella was starting to panic and when you panic, you use a lot of breath. Steve and Bob tried to keep calm about it, but were finding it very hard. I, Nicky, was keeping calm as I had to control the rocket. I had to dodge lots of things. Then all of a sudden, a meteoroid started to head this way. *Boom!*

Lacy-Mai Bollen (11)
Wyedean School, Sedbury

Life On A Heated Earth

It's been weeks since it started. The sun's glaring through the window of the flat that I use for shelter. It feels like a billion volcanic eruptions have heated the Earth. This is all because of the sun. My life sucks! If you think your life is bad, times it by ten, and it still won't be as bad as mine. About half of the population are dead, and it's not going to get any better. I really miss my family. I feel sick, I don't feel well at all. I think about my family as the end closes in.

Matthew Whitcombe (11)
Wyedean School, Sedbury

The Eruption

There had been a volcano eruption in Hollywood. Who would survive it? As I walked through the devastating volcano eruption, I could see loads of bodies, they were all dead. I found only two people throughout this eruption and their names were Aimo and Thomas. We went through this cave, and we soon discovered that the dead bodies turned into lava zombies. We found these guns and killed them to discover an amazing city, it had a massive wall so the zombies couldn't enter it. Maybe we could climb over it.

Ethan Dash (12)
Wyedean School, Sedbury

The War Against Venus

Here we are, on our way to Venus to fight this war. I don't know how we are going to win against these aliens. No one knows anything about them, so we just have to hope that luck is on our side. Here we are, approaching the planet, it looks like they're not here yet... So we have time to set up and get armour on. We see their ship approaching, they jump off and all I see is a green light. That's when the mothership arrives. It charges up and then shoots a gargantuan laser into Earth.

Todd Michael Thomas (11)
Wyedean School, Sedbury

It's Time!

It was time! Every year, the door opened to the other world. People had been out there but never returned.
A strange man sitting on the edge wall said, "It's like a maze out there, beware, it's not for fun."
I was pushed through the door, doing the walk of shame. It was pitch-black. I knew that I had to find my way out, I had to place my hand on the wall and keep going. All I had in my backpack was water and a knife. *These may be my last hours.* Was I really free?

Liam Morgan (12)
Wyedean School, Sedbury

The Blue City

I was walking through the lovely city of New York. I walked back into my apartment. I turned the TV on. There was a newsflash saying, "Run, get out of the city, quick, and run for your life!"
It was a flood that was heading to the city. It said that it was terrible but I didn't believe it so I carried on with my day.
The next morning, there was something strange. I went into the living room and saw the water rising. I was trapped in the apartment. The water was rising fast.

Evie Rose Hunter (12)
Wyedean School, Sedbury

The Only Survivor

I stepped outside. This was my world turned upside down. After the heatwave, a wildfire began. It took the lives of all my family. I was the only one left now, with nothing to live for, nowhere to run to, and nowhere to shelter. So I ran, no place to be and no place to go. I came across a river, full of ash and rubble from buildings. My heart was broken to see this damage. I realised this river contained the victims of the fires. I threw myself in. We were a family once more, reunited and happy...

Olivia Abigail Legg (11)
Wyedean School, Sedbury

Sinkhole

After the war, nukes were set off, mutating all the animals and turning people psycho. Seven billion dead already. The world was covered with dead corpses all over. Food was limited, London was just a big pile of rubble. In the distance, there was a group of three-headed dogs eating the five-legged elephants. If you went outside, they would get you. I had a little dug out under the rubble, where I would sleep. I found out I had no more food, so I needed to hurry. I went out and I sank, falling.

Jonah Ford (13)
Wyedean School, Sedbury

Untitled

It was a normal summer day, I was going to work and I heard the alarm for a disaster. A billboard overhead read: *Danger! Heatwave, stay inside!* It was up there for about two minutes, then it cut off. I knelt down and touched the floor, it was burning. I looked up at the billboard, it seemed to be tipping over so I ran away. The further I got, the more I could smell burning. I stopped, looked behind me and saw everything burning, including the path ahead. I was trapped in a wildfire...

Murray King (11)
Wyedean School, Sedbury

The Lava Run

My tired, wary legs cried out for help, desperate to stop. I had to keep going, it felt like I had been running for eternity. The heat burnt my back, it was like the lava was chasing me. I was so thirsty, my mouth was so dry. I could see the steps, the steps to my safety. If only I could keep going, but the lava appeared to be gaining on me. I looked back in panic, my heart was pounding, my breath was shallow. I stumbled, falling to the ground. Exhaustion took over, I could not get back up...

Harriet Tyldesley (11)
Wyedean School, Sedbury

Disaster Of The Desert

Three weeks in. Joe and I have been scouting Newport, our greatest threat. Suddenly, I see a bunch of rats surrounding a dig site. A sudden feeling in my spine makes me shiver, as I get back in. Immediately, twenty or so people from Newport appear, dashing at us madly. I pull out my knife and yell my war cry. Suddenly, I begin charging forward, as quick as I can. I roll over and cut someone's hamstring and they fall to the floor. I look up to see a grenade. Is this my harsh brutal end?

Alexander Catlin (12)
Wyedean School, Sedbury

Thermal

The air seems more boiling than usual, making my skin peel and my lungs burst into flames with every gulp of oxygen I take. Around me stand ash models of humans and stone from buildings that have started to go molten. The sun has moved too close to Earth. Now cities lie in sand and corpses. The only way we are going to survive is if we get to a thermal bunker. Only then we can hope. This is only the unthinkable, the exact opposite of an ice age. Only the strongest will survive.

Jack Qualter Buncall (12)
Wyedean School, Sedbury

After The Quake

So that's it. My family's never coming back. The earthquake tore my family apart. Quite literally. The small town that I have called home for eleven years is now gone. The park where I used to play with my brother, the coffee shop my mother and father used to run, my grandparents' luxury flat, it has all gone. My home, my memories, my life. What I want to know is why did this happen? Where will I live? Who will look after me? Why am I the only one surviving?

Abi Giles (11)
Wyedean School, Sedbury

Underwater

It's been years, but everyone knows that it's how we have to live now... Jas and I swam through the deep, blue, unending sea of the world. We then climbed onto my floating house.

I suddenly exclaimed, "Jas, look at your leg, you have scales!"

We quickly ran to tell my mum and when we were telling her, I noticed that she had scales on her leg, as did I. Then Dad came downstairs and he had scales too. Suddenly, Jaz and I knew where to go...

Izzy Robb (11)
Wyedean School, Sedbury

The Hurricane Hit!

I can't remember what the world was like before it happened. They told us we were going to be okay. But then the hurricane hit. I couldn't believe my eyes. After a while, I was worried and scared as all of my belongings were left behind and the only shelter I had was destroyed by the big hit. As I was alone, I thought, *what should I do?* I ran as fast as I could to get away from the frightening shock. My heart thumped as I ran faster and faster...

Rhia Admans (12)
Wyedean School, Sedbury

Reincarnated

As I got out of my car, I heard nothing but silence. I had a feeling of uncertainty. I knew I had to go in. All of the glass was smashed, sprawled across the floor. The windows were bare and soulless. I looked on the floor below the kiosk. A man in a black tuxedo lay on the floor, covered in blood. I flipped his face, he looked lifeless. I prodded him in his arm and it twitched. I jumped back and I gathered enough courage to prod him one more time. He was alive!

William Tett (12)
Wyedean School, Sedbury

The Last Survivor

I stared out at the eerie land I used to call home. I looked at my house, all crumbled and in despair. I walked along the streets of my once lovely town and called the names of my loving parents. Nobody answered except the gentle breeze. I was alone in a land I used to know and call my own. I dropped to my knees miserably, I was well and truly alone. I looked around for someone, anyone, but I was the last survivor. The last person to walk on the Earth...

Phoebe Jones (12)
Wyedean School, Sedbury

The Button That Changed The World

Beep! Just like that, all the world wiped from existence. I ran, with a Zeko running behind me. It was a fight for survival. Those with guns could kill the Zekos (huge creatures with huge fangs), so to protect yourself you needed guns. You could get food and water. For people like me, it was more difficult. You had to put yourself in danger. For food, I ran up to a Zeko nest and stole one of their eggs. It was easy if they didn't see you.

Fraser Rickards (11)
Wyedean School, Sedbury

Rising Heat

It was a day where the clouds were in the blue sky. No one knew a storm was brewing at the top of the mountain. Something had happened, but what? The Earth started to spin. Leaves started to set on fire, all ice and metal set on fire. The heat had risen in under one hour. Why, all of a sudden, had all the mountains started to throw lava out? Water turned into steam. I didn't know what to do, where was it safe to stay?

Will Haywood (11)
Wyedean School, Sedbury

YOUNG WRITERS INFORMATION

We hope you have enjoyed reading this book – and that you will continue to in the coming years.

If you're a young writer who enjoys reading and creative writing, or the parent of an enthusiastic poet or story writer, do visit our website **www.youngwriters.co.uk**. Here you will find free competitions, workshops and games, as well as recommended reads, a poetry glossary and our blog.

If you would like to order further copies of this book, or any of our other titles, then please give us a call or order via your online account.

Young Writers
Remus House
Coltsfoot Drive
Peterborough
PE2 9BF
(01733) 890066 / 898110
info@youngwriters.co.uk

Join in the conversation!

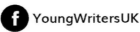 YoungWritersUK    @YoungWritersCW